Sam the Stolen Puppy

Other Holly Webb books
available from Stripes:

Sam the Stolen Puppy

Holly Webb

Illustrated by Sophy Williams

stripes

For Emily Ruby,
and for Robin and William

STRIPES PUBLISHING
An imprint of Magi Publications
1 The Coda Centre, 189 Munster Road,
London SW6 6AW

A paperback original
First published in Great Britain in 2008

Text copyright © Holly Webb, 2008
Illustrations copyright © Sophy Williams, 2008

ISBN-13: 978-1-84715-041-7

A CIP catalogue record for this book is available
from the British Library.

Printed and bound in Germany

10 9 8 7 6 5 4 3 2 1

Chapter One

The living room was covered in shreds of wrapping paper, and Emily's mum was desperately trying to keep track. "Emily, was that toy car Jack just opened from Auntie May or Auntie Sue? No, hang on, Auntie Sue sent you both book tokens, didn't she?" She stared at the list, anxiously. "But I'm sure she said something about a car."

Emily's dad rustled through the paper to try and find a gift tag. "No, sorry, I think Jack's eaten it."

"Is it breakfast?" Jack had caught on to the idea of food. "I want toast!" He abandoned the car in a pile of paper and ribbon, and started to head for the kitchen.

"Hey! Come back here!" Dad called, a little crossly.

Jack turned back, looking confused. "But I thought breakfast..." he said, in a hurt voice.

Dad picked him up, and tickled him. "Sorry, Jack, I didn't mean to sound cross. We just need to wait a bit. Emily hasn't opened all her presents yet. Come on, Emily – you're not usually so slow."

Emily was sitting quietly with a neat pile of opened presents next to her. They were nice. A pair of new trainers. A pink fluffy winter hat and scarf. New glitter pens and a sketchpad. She *should* be happy. But she couldn't help being a tiny bit disappointed. There had only been one thing on her Christmas list.

She and Jack had both written letters to Father Christmas – well, Emily had written Jack's for him, which took for ever, because he kept changing his mind, and he wanted most of the toy shop in his stocking. He'd drawn a big spiky thing he said was a reindeer, and a J at the bottom, which was all he could manage, because he was only just three. Dad had lit the fire in the grate, even though it wasn't really that cold, and they'd sent the letters flying up the chimney in a rush of flickering ashes. Emily wasn't convinced about letters magically racing to the North Pole, but it was still fun to do. And you never knew, anyway…

Still, she hadn't really expected Father Christmas to leave a puppy at the end of her bed. It had been a big hint to Mum and Dad, and they seemed to have missed it. Emily had one present left, and it certainly didn't have a dog in it. It was far too small. Though it did have very cute wrapping paper – silver, with little black pawprints scattered all over it.

"Sorry, Jack, I've just got this one to open." Trying not to look too disappointed, Emily carefully tore the end of the parcel – she wanted to keep the pawprint paper. She couldn't work out what was inside as she peered in. She'd guessed from the shape that it might be clothes, even though it felt a bit hard. She shook the parcel, and out came something red, uncoiling itself as it came. A red dog collar, and a lead!

Emily's tummy turned over with hope and trying-not-to-get-too-excited-because-it-might-not-mean-what-she-thought-it-meant. She *did* have a very gorgeous toy Dalmatian dog called Georgie, who was almost life-size. Until a couple of years ago, one of her favourite games had been to pretend that he was real, and tie ribbons round his neck for a lead.

But she never did that now. Almost never, anyway. Mum and Dad wouldn't have bought her a real collar and lead just for Georgie, would they?

Slowly, she looked up at her parents, the collar lying in her hands, like it was something incredibly precious.

Her dad was grinning. "Can anyone hear something in the kitchen?" he asked thoughtfully. "I'm sure there's a noise. Maybe in the utility room. Sort of a *barking* noise…"

Emily leaped up in excitement and rushed to the kitchen door, and then through to the little room at the end where they kept the washing machine. In the corner of the room was a beautiful new basket. Emily knelt down beside it, hardly breathing, she was so excited. The basket was padded with a soft fleecy blanket, and snuggled into one corner of it was a ball of golden fur. As Emily watched, the puppy heaved a great sigh that seemed to go from one end of its body to the other, and then opened one eye to peer up at her. Obviously she looked interesting, because the other eye opened too, and then the tiny dog turned round and stood up. He gave a massive yawn, showing a lot of pink tongue and some very sharp little white teeth, then padded across the basket to reach Emily. They were almost nose to nose. The puppy gave a shy little wag of his tail, and licked Emily's cheek, looking at her hopefully. This looked like someone who might be good at cuddling. It had been a little bit boring tucked away in this basket.

"Oh, wow…" Very gently, Emily put out her hand for the puppy to sniff. She was desperate to pick him up, but she wasn't sure if it was OK. Maybe the puppy would be scared? She looked round to see Dad leaning against the door, looking pleased.

"That's really good, Emily. Taking it slow. That's just what you need to do." He crouched down by the basket too. "Pet him a little. Stroke his ears. Then when he's used to that you can give him a cuddle."

"He's really for me?" Emily whispered, hardly able to take her eyes off the puppy.

"All yours." Dad was grinning as he watched Emily's amazed face.

"He's so beautiful, thank you so much, Dad! I didn't think you'd noticed I wanted a dog."

"It would have been hard *not* to notice," Dad said, laughing. "You certainly gave us some hints! Dogs just seemed to keep being mentioned…"

"He's a golden Labrador, isn't he? He's so lovely. You are the most beautiful dog I've ever seen," Emily murmured, as she tickled the puppy behind his ears with one finger. His ears felt like velvet, so soft. The puppy closed his eyes in delight. Just the right place. One of his back legs kicked without him meaning it to, as Emily tickled a really itchy bit.

Emily looked worriedly up at Dad. "Did I do something wrong? Why did he do that with his leg?"

"No, it's OK. Some dogs do that. My dog Scruff used to do it whenever you scratched him behind the ears. It just means they like it, and they want more scratching. Don't you, hmmm? And you're right, he is a golden Labrador," he added, reaching out to stroke the puppy too. "He's eight weeks old." He grinned down at Emily, who was still gazing in wonder at the puppy, stroking him with one finger. "So you like him then?"

"I love him!" Emily wanted to leap up

and hug him, but she didn't want to frighten the puppy with any sudden movements.

"Good," said Dad. "Why don't you try picking him up? That's it, scoop him up gently. Make sure you're supporting his bottom so he feels comfortable."

Emily carefully snuggled the puppy into her dressing gown, and the little dog immediately tried to climb up her front, eager to explore.

"Take him into the kitchen," Dad suggested. "Let him have a little look around. I went and picked him up late last night, and we've kept him in here since then. He needs to settle in to the house gradually. Just a room at a time. We'll keep him in here and the kitchen for now."

Emily stood up, very, very carefully, and walked slowly into the kitchen, the puppy peering round her shoulder. The little dog's bright black eyes were taking everything in.

Mum and Jack were sitting at the kitchen table, and Jack was wolfing down a big bowl of cereal. As he saw Emily walk in, his eyes went wide, and a spoonful of milk dribbled out of his mouth.

"That's a dog!" he gasped.

"Yes," Mum agreed. "He's Emily's. For Christmas. But I'm sure Emily will let you play with him too."

Jack started to bounce up and down on his chair, laughing with excitement. "A dog! A dog a dog a dog a dog a dog a dog!"

"Watch it!" Mum reached over, and removed his cereal bowl to a safe distance. "Calm down, Jack." She handed him a cloth, which he ignored entirely, still staring at the puppy.

"Why did Emily get a puppy and not me?" he asked, frowning.

"You're a little bit young for your own puppy, darling," Mum explained. "Father Christmas brought you a remote control train."

Jack looked unconvinced. "I'd like a dog more," he muttered.

Emily sat down on the very edge of a chair with the puppy in her lap. "He's so lovely," she murmured. "I can't believe you really gave me a dog!" Suddenly she sat up a little straighter, clutching at the puppy to stop him falling. "What about that TV ad?" she said worriedly. "I saw it after I wrote my Christmas letter. It said you shouldn't give dogs as presents."

Mum and Dad exchanged looks. "It's

true, Emily, it's not really the best idea," Mum said. "People often think a cute little puppy would be a lovely present, and then when the puppy gets bigger, they don't want the work of looking after it properly."

"Because it is a lot of work, Emily, you're going to need to be really responsible," Dad put in.

Emily nodded seriously. She would be super-responsible!

"But we were planning to get you a dog anyway," Mum went on. "We'd already contacted the people who bred your puppy, and we were waiting for the next litter of pups to come along. This little one just happened to arrive at the right time to be the perfect Christmas present."

Emily hardly ate any Christmas lunch. She kept disappearing from the table to check on the puppy. He had a little bit of turkey, and some carrots, but Dad said he couldn't have any Christmas pudding.

"And Emily, you really mustn't give him anything from the table. We don't want him learning to jump up and steal food!" Mum got up to start clearing the plates. "Have you thought of a name for him yet?" she asked, as she went over to the sink.

Emily looked thoughtfully at the puppy, who was having a fight with a piece of wrapping paper, rolling over with it and growling. "I think I'm going to call him Sam," she decided. "He looks like a Sam."

"That's a nice sensible name," Dad agreed. "We don't want to be yelling, 'Here, Fluffikins!' across the park, do we?"

Emily giggled. "Actually, I think Fluffikins is a cool name, Dad, thanks!" She knelt down next to the puppy. "You'd like to be called Fluffikins, wouldn't you?"

The puppy made a disgusted noise, and spat out a small ball of wrapping paper at her.

Emily grinned. "OK, Sam it is, then." She leaned forward, resting her chin on her hand, watching the puppy nosing around her feet, sniffing and snorting quietly to himself. Then he climbed on to her foot and looked up at her hopefully, one paw in the air. Emily giggled. "Hey, Sam," she said, reaching down to pick him up.

Sam gave a delighted sigh, and firmly stamped up and down on Emily's lap until it was just right. Then he flopped down and fell fast asleep in seconds.

Emily watched his tiny body twitching as he slept. She still couldn't believe he was hers. How could anyone be so lucky?

Chapter Two

The Christmas holidays seemed to race past even faster than usual with Sam to play with. In no time at all, Emily was back at school. She spent the first day worrying about what he might be doing, and whether he was lonely without her. When Mum and Jack came to pick her up, Emily raced ahead. Mum had to keep calling to her to slow down.

"Come on, Jack!" Emily called crossly, as he stopped again. He was counting snails, and it took ages to get anywhere. Emily was desperate to get home and see Sam, she'd really missed him. It didn't help that Jack had spent most of the walk so far chatting away about what a fun time *he'd* had playing with Sam while Emily was at school. It wasn't fair. Sam was *her* puppy! But Emily supposed she couldn't really say Jack wasn't allowed to play with him. Actually, in a way she was glad that Jack had been there, because otherwise Sam might have been lonely. She just hoped that Sam had missed her a little bit!

Back at the house, Sam was padding about, feeling confused. He hadn't seen Emily in ages. She'd been away before, but never for this long. He didn't understand about school, even though Emily had explained it all very carefully the night before and promised him that she would be back.

Sam sniffed carefully under the sofa, in case Emily was hiding there. No, just a lot of fluff and some Lego bricks. He sneezed. Then he trotted out into the hallway, and gazed up at the stairs. He couldn't quite manage the stairs yet, and he wondered if she was up there. But normally, if Emily was going upstairs, she took him with her.

Sam whined, and then tried a hopeful little bark. No Emily came running. He sat down and rested his nose on the first step, tired from searching. It had been quite fun playing with the little boy, but it wasn't the same. He wanted Emily back, she was his special person.

Emily hopped about on the doorstep, waiting for Mum and Jack to catch up. Why were they taking so long? She dropped her school bag and knelt down to peer through the letter box, hoping to catch a glimpse of Sam.

"Ohhh!" There he was, flopped down next to the stairs, fast asleep.

"Emily, what are you doing?" Mum asked, as she and Jack came up the path.

"Looking at Sam, he's so cute, he's fallen asleep..."

They opened the door very quietly and crept in, shushing Jack, who wouldn't stop chattering.

Sam heard the door click shut and sprang up, barking excitedly. She was back! He was so excited he ran round Emily in circles, jumping on all four paws and squeaking to show her how happy he was.

Emily picked him up, and he licked her all over, desperate to welcome her back.

Emily kissed the top of his head, rubbing her cheek over the soft golden fur. "I can hardly hold him, he's wagging his tail so hard," she giggled.

"I think he might just have missed you a little bit," Mum said, with her head on one side, pretending to think about it.

Emily smiled to herself. She didn't want Sam to be sad, but it was nice to know he'd missed her too.

It wasn't long before Sam was old enough to go out for walks. He loved it, and so did Emily. The problem was, Sam got so excited by being outside that he spent the whole time barking and yelping and jumping up and down, so that by the time they got home he was so tired Emily had to carry him.

"I think Sam needs some dog-training classes," Dad said, as he watched Sam running in his sleep after a particularly exciting walk one weekend. He'd tied his lead in a knot round Emily's ankles, and then pulled her over when he went racing after a squirrel.

Emily nodded, but she looked a little anxious. "Will they be very difficult classes?" she asked.

"No, don't worry, I'm not suggesting we train him to jump through hoops or anything. Just the basics. How to walk nicely on the lead, sit, stay, that kind of thing."

"Ohhh." Emily brightened up. That did sound very useful. Sam was gorgeous, and great fun to take for walks, but he wore her out too.

Dad found out that there was a dog-training class held in the local park on a Saturday morning, which was perfect. It meant he and Emily could take Sam together. Now that she knew they wouldn't have to do anything too hard, Emily was very excited about it. She begged Mum to buy a special packet of puppy treats to take with them for when Sam did really well.

Jack was very upset that he wasn't allowed to go, even though Mum promised that he could do something special with her. He threw a massive tantrum on Saturday morning, and Emily felt a tiny bit guilty. Jack really did love Sam too.

"I suppose we could all go," she told Dad as they walked down the front path with Jack staring out of the window after them, tears still trickling down his face.

Dad shook his head. "That's sweet of you, Emily, but Jack's too young. This class is for us almost more than it is for Sam – teaching *us* how to teach *him*. We wouldn't be able to concentrate on the class properly if Jack was with us. He'd never stop chatting!"

Emily giggled. Dad was right. Maybe she could hold a special dog-training class in the garden later, and show Jack what they'd learned.

The park was very close, but Emily was feeling tired by the time they got there. Sam seemed to want to do anything except walk in a straight line. He definitely needed training!

Luckily, Lucy, the instructor, was very nice, and she reckoned that Sam would soon get the hang of it.

"You're starting young, which is exactly right. He's a lovely little dog," she said, patting Sam. Lucy thought it was best for Emily to do the training, and Dad to watch and help out. "It'll be easier if he has one person in charge, then he won't get confused," she explained.

Emily had been looking forward to telling Mum and Jack everything they'd done, but when they got home, Jack wasn't interested. "Don't want to see," he muttered, when Emily tried to show him how Sam walked to heel.

Mum gave her an apologetic look. "Still grumpy," she mouthed, and sighed. "So, the class went all right then? Did Sam do as he was told?"

Dad and Emily exchanged an

embarrassed look. "*Some* of the time," Emily said. "He did stay for a little while, but he wasn't very good at the bit where he was supposed to sit and look at a dog biscuit, and not eat it until he was told. He had four!"

Sam sat under the kitchen table, panting to himself and showing all his teeth in a big doggy grin. He *liked* dog-training...

Jack sulked about the dog-training all weekend, but on Monday morning he suddenly brightened up. He seemed very eager for Emily to get off to school and leave him alone with Sam.

Emily couldn't help wondering just what Jack was planning. It was obviously something to do with Sam. She got told off twice by her class teacher for not paying attention, and the second time he was really cross. So she wasn't in a very good mood when Mum and Jack came to pick her up, and she got even grumpier when she saw Jack's smug face.

"What have you been doing?" she growled. "You'd better not have spent all day messing around with Sam. He's *my* dog!"

"Emily!" her mum said. "That's not very nice!"

Emily stared at the ground, feeling even more annoyed with Jack.

Jack just beamed at her. "I'm doing dog-training too!" he announced proudly.

"Jack's coming to dog-training?" Emily gave her mum a hurt look. "But Dad said—"

"Not your dog-training. That's boring. *My* dog-training. I'm teaching Sam how to sing." And Jack danced along the pavement, singing loudly to himself.

Emily sighed. Jack was so silly sometimes. "He'd have to be better than you!" she called after her brother.

Emily and her mum expected Jack's singing lessons to last about a day, but surprisingly, he kept going. Every so often he would disappear off with Sam, and he got very huffy if anyone tried to join in.

Then one Friday afternoon, when Dad got home, Jack appeared in the kitchen looking very pleased with himself.

"Me an' Sam have got something to show you!" he said, excitedly.

Mum and Emily exchanged a look. "Is this your singing?" Mum asked kindly.

Jack nodded. "You all have to listen. Sit down, Daddy," he ordered.

Dad had been putting the kettle on, but he grinned, and found a chair. "Go on then. Where's the star?"

Jack opened the kitchen door, and peered round. "Sam! Sammy! C'mon!"

Sam pattered in.

"Everybody ssshhhh!" Jack hissed. He sat down on the floor with Sam, and started to sing "Row, Row, Row Your Boat".

Sam wagged his tail, lifted his nose up to the ceiling and barked along. "Ruff, ruff, ruff-ruff-ruff..."

When they finished, with a long howl from Sam, there was a stunned silence in the kitchen.

"Did I just imagine that?" Dad asked.

Emily shook her head. "No, he really did it!" She knelt down to make a big fuss of Sam. "You're such a clever boy! I can't believe you taught him that, Jack, that's brilliant!"

"We're going to learn 'The Grand Old Duke of York' next," Jack said, pleased with the reaction he'd got. "But it's a bit harder."

The real dog-training classes started to go a lot better after the first couple of weeks – it was as though Sam suddenly got the hang of it. Emily felt really proud of him at the classes. He was so little compared to some of the other dogs, but he was one of the best ones there.

"Sam, sit!" Emily was standing just in front of him. Sam looked up at her enquiringly. Oh yes, he knew this one. He thumped his bottom down, tail swishing the grass happily.

"Good boy! Now, stay!" Emily turned and walked away.

Sam watched her uncertainly. He wanted to follow Emily, but he knew he wasn't supposed to. He gave a little whine, hoping she might come back to him.

Emily looked round. "Stay, Sam!" she said firmly.

Sam sighed, and watched Emily with his head on one side, waiting. Yes! Now she was calling him. He leaped up and raced towards her, frisking round her legs happily.

"He's doing really well, Emily, you've worked hard with him." Lucy, the class instructor, was smiling down at Sam. "You gorgeous boy." She tickled him under the chin, and Sam closed his eyes blissfully. "Right, everyone, we're going to practise that a few more times."

Emily told Sam to sit again, and walked back to the other side of the training area. Sam waited beautifully, and Emily glowed with pride. Quite a few people were standing with Dad, watching the class, and she imagined them all thinking how well behaved he was. One couple seemed particularly interested in the dogs, and Emily was sure she saw them point to Sam. They had a gorgeous pointer with them. Maybe they wanted to bring him to the class, although he looked a bit old. As Emily watched, the pointer half-turned to look at a dog walking behind him, and the man who was holding his lead yanked him back really hard.

The dog crouched back against the man's legs with his shoulders hunched, looking miserable, and Emily gasped. That was so mean!

The man caught her watching, and smiled at her. Emily looked away quickly. She'd almost forgotten Sam, and she turned back to call him.

Sam had got a bit bored waiting, and he thought Emily had forgotten him too. He was creeping very slowly towards her on his bottom, with a "please don't tell me off!" look on his face.

Emily giggled. He was so funny!

Emily soon stopped thinking about the couple with the pointer, she was too busy concentrating on Sam. At the end of the class Dad was full of praise for them both, and they were all walking happily back to the park gates when Sam turned round and yapped. The pointer was right behind him, and he wanted to say hello.

"Oh, sorry," Dad said to the man holding him. "Is your dog friendly? Sam hasn't met that many other dogs yet, he gets a bit excited."

Emily glared. That wasn't fair. Sam *did* like meeting other dogs, but they shouldn't have been letting their pointer get that close if they didn't want Sam to talk to him.

"Don't worry! Bertie's very friendly," the man said, smiling.

Emily didn't think the pointer looked that friendly. He looked as though he was too scared of being told off to do *anything*. He cowered away from the man, and something about the man's too-nice voice made Emily shiver. She didn't trust him.

"Your puppy is gorgeous," the woman who was with him said. "Is he a pedigree Labrador?"

Dad said that Sam was indeed a pedigree dog, and mentioned the breeder he'd come from. The couple seemed very interested, and asked lots of friendly questions, but Emily still didn't like them. She tugged at Dad's hand, hoping to get him to leave, but he ignored her.

"Da-aaad… Can we go?" Emily muttered.

Dad looked down at her in surprise. "Wait a minute, Emily, we're just chatting." He frowned at her in a way that said "Behave!" and Emily scowled back. Couldn't Dad see these weren't nice people?

The woman crouched down to stroke Sam, and he backed away up against Emily and growled.

"Sam!" Dad sounded shocked, but Emily was glad. She didn't want them touching him!

The woman smiled. "Don't worry," she said. "I probably smell of Bertie, and he doesn't like it."

Sam huddled close to Emily, still growling, but faintly so that only she could hear him. The woman didn't smell of Bertie, she smelled of lots of dogs. Lots of *unhappy* dogs, and he didn't want to be anywhere near her. He didn't want to end up like Bertie.

Dad and Emily set off for home with Sam trotting along, walking to heel, like he'd been taught. Occasionally Emily had to remind him, but not very often.

Dad wasn't noticing how well Sam was doing though. "Emily, that was very rude just now. You know better than that. What on earth's the matter with you?"

Emily shrugged. It sounded a bit stupid, now they'd left the strange couple behind. "They just didn't seem very nice," she muttered. "I didn't like them being so interested in Sam."

"Emily, those people were perfectly nice. Don't be so silly," Dad snapped.

"But Sam didn't like them either!" Emily protested. "Dogs are good at telling what people are really like!"

"Sam just picked up on your bad behaviour," Dad said sternly. "I don't want either of you being like that again. Now let's get home."

Emily walked along, glaring at the pavement as they turned into their road. Dad was being unfair, she was sure. She knew she was right not to trust them.

Sam looked up at her anxiously, sensing that something was wrong. Then suddenly the fur prickled on the back of his neck, and he looked behind him. His low growl jolted Emily out of her sulk, and she turned to see what Sam had seen.

The couple with the pointer were just walking past the end of Emily's road, watching them...

Chapter Three

Now that Sam was walking so well on the lead, Mum let Emily take him on their walk to school on Monday morning. She said it wouldn't be every day, though, she couldn't cope with Sam *and* Jack!

They met lots of Emily's school friends on the way, and they all fussed over Sam.

"He's so cute!" Emily's friend Ruby murmured, stroking Sam behind his ears. "You're so lucky, Emily, my parents would never let me have a dog."

Emily grinned, and gave Mum a quick, grateful look. She knew she was lucky. Then she stiffened, her heart jumping in surprise. It was those people again! The ones with Bertie! The Watsons, Dad had said they were called. She watched as they walked past on the other side of the road. Bertie looked even more sad than he had on Saturday – his head hung low and his tail drooped.

"What's the matter, Emily?" Mum asked curiously, watching them too.

"N-nothing…" Emily didn't want to sound silly, especially not with Ruby there. "I just saw someone from dog-training, that's all." She supposed they had every right to walk around the town. Maybe they just happened to live in a street near school, and Emily's house, and the park… But she still had the strangest feeling that they were watching her. And Sam.

Emily tried not to worry about the man and woman with the pointer. Dad had been so sure she was being silly. But she couldn't help looking over her shoulder every so often on the walk home from school, and the drive to her ballet class.

She gave Sam an extra-big cuddle that night as they settled down to sleep. Mum had been a bit worried about Sam sleeping on Emily's bed, but he was really well house-trained now – and he howled if he was left downstairs! Emily was sure she slept much better with Sam curled up on her toes, although Dad had commented that they might need to get her a bigger bed when Sam was a fully-grown dog!

Sam loved sleeping on Emily's bed, and he was quite certain that his basket was only for daytime naps. There was no way he was going to let Emily sleep without him guarding her.

That night, Sam was snoozing happily when his comfy nest of duvet suddenly wriggled. He opened one eye sleepily, and it wriggled again. This time he sat up and let out an indignant little woof. What was Emily doing? All he could see of her was a huddle of covers. He padded gently further up the bed to investigate.

Emily was muttering and moaning in her sleep, hitting at her pillow with her hands. Anxiously, Sam whined in her ear, trying to wake her up, but she didn't notice him. Sam looked worriedly at her for a moment. Something was obviously wrong. He stuck his cold wet nose in the hollow under Emily's chin, knowing that would wake her.

"Oh!" Emily sat up, looking relieved and scared at the same time. She hugged Sam. "Oh, Sam, that was horrible. I was having a really weird dream, about those people we saw in the park." She shuddered, and Sam licked her sympathetically. He didn't really understand what she meant, but she was obviously upset.

Emily shook her head, feeling dazed. She couldn't remember the dream properly, just confused mind-pictures of lots of dogs barking sadly. But she knew it had been horrible, and she didn't want to remember any more.

Sam snuggled up against her, trying to tell her that it would be all right.

"Oh, Sam..." Sleepily, Emily lay back down. "I do love you."

Sam *did* understand that. Emily said it lots, and he knew it was very important.

I love you too, he told her firmly. *And I'll always be here. Now go to sleep.* And this time he curled up by her shoulder, determined that nothing was going to hurt her, not while he was there to look after her.

But when Emily got home from school the next day, Sam wasn't rushing down the hall to see her. Usually he met her at the door, barking delightedly, and wanting to be made a fuss of, but today there was no whirling, barking ball of golden fur. Emily checked upstairs while Mum tried to get Jack out of his coat. When she came back down, Mum had started making their tea, and was trying to explain to Jack why he couldn't have fish fingers every day, and it had to be pasta sometimes. She didn't really notice when Emily dashed out into the garden to look for Sam.

Sam wasn't there. Emily hadn't really

expected him to be – Mum wouldn't have left him out in the garden while she went to collect her from school – but she'd been getting a bit desperate. Sam wasn't upstairs, and he definitely wasn't downstairs, so if he wasn't in the garden, *where was he?*

"Mum, I can't find Sam!" Emily burst out, as she raced back into the kitchen.

"Don't bang the door like that, Emily!" Mum said, with her head in the fridge.

"Sorry, but Mum, where's Sam?"

"I should think he's upstairs, having a sleep. I *think* that's where he was when we left." Mum still wasn't really paying attention. "Or in the garden, maybe?"

"I've just looked in the garden!"

Emily grabbed her mum's arm, desperate to make her listen. "He's not upstairs either, I've looked. He's not anywhere, Mum!"

"He must be…" Mum was actually paying attention now, but she didn't seem to realize how serious this was. "He's probably got shut in one of the rooms by accident, while I was vacuuming. Go and check all the bedrooms, Emily."

Jack looked round from the table, where he was playing with his toy diggers. "No, Mummy, Sam's with the lady," he said helpfully.

Emily and Mum turned to stare at him, and Emily gasped in horror. "What lady?" she asked, barely able to speak.

Jack just shrugged. "The one that came to borrow Sam. When you were upstairs, Mummy."

Mum knelt down by Jack's chair and tried to get him to explain, but it was hard to get him to give any more details. He'd been riding his trike in the garden, and the lady had come in through the back gate. She'd said she was just borrowing Sam and she'd bring him back later.

"What did she look like?" Emily asked. "Tell me!"

"Just a lady!" Jack was sounding a bit cross and scared now. He didn't understand why Emily was so angry with him, and Mum looked so panicked. "Oh!" He remembered something helpful. "She had red gloves," he told Emily happily. "Sam didn't like them, he tried to bite them." He smiled at Emily, hoping she'd be pleased with him now, but she was crying, and he started to cry too. "When is the lady bringing Sam back?" he asked, miserably. "Mummy, when is Sam coming back?"

Emily's mum phoned the police. It took ages, and she kept being put through to different people, but Emily and Jack stood next to her, listening hard and trying to work out what was happening. At last she put the phone down, and beckoned them over to sit on the sofa with her.

"Emily, the policeman I was just talking to, he's in charge of an investigation at the moment. There's – well, they think there's a gang of what are called dog-nappers working in this area at the moment."

"Dog-nappers?" Emily hadn't ever heard the word before. Jack was just listening, wide-eyed and still teary.

Emily wouldn't talk to him, and he wanted Sam to come back, and he was miserable.

"Like kidnappers for dogs," Mum said slowly, putting an arm round each of them. "Lots of pedigree dogs have gone missing round here recently, especially young dogs."

"But what happens to them?" Emily whispered. She was still trying to understand what was going on – someone had stolen Sam!

Mum looked upset. She took Emily's hand. "The policeman's going to come round and ask us about what happened. We can ask him questions too."

It should have been exciting, having a policeman coming to their house, like being part of an adventure story,

The Case of the Stolen Dogs. But it wasn't. Emily would much rather have had Sam back and no adventure at all.

Jack was thrilled to have a real police car outside the house at first, but then the policeman wanted to ask him what had happened when Sam was taken, and he went completely shy and wouldn't say anything. Emily felt like screaming at him – she was furious that he'd just sat there on his trike while Sam got stolen, and now he wouldn't even help!

The policeman made notes about what Sam looked like, and said it was good that they'd let him know quickly. "But he's a valuable dog, I'm afraid, and being so young as well, he's going to be very easy for them to sell on."

Emily looked at him, confused. "But we'll get him back before he gets sold, won't we? You'll find him."

The policeman just looked sad, and gave a funny sort of cough.

Mum didn't say anything for a moment. Then she hugged Emily tighter.

"Emily, the police will do their best, of course, but the dog-nappers are very well organized. The gang seem to be able to make dogs just disappear."

Emily swallowed. "So – we might never get Sam back…?" Tears rolled down her face, and her nose started to run. She didn't care. She stared at the policeman, who looked so out of place in their living room. "You mean we might never see him again?"

Chapter Four

Shut away in the dark, Sam howled for Emily to come and find him. This was far worse than being left at home while they all went off to school, and playgroup, and shopping. He padded anxiously around the little wire pen, sniffing the strange smells. There were other dogs here. Sam could hear them, barking and whining, angry about being shut up in their pens. He was sure that there had been at least five different dogs living in this pen before him, too. He just didn't understand why.

One thing Sam was certain of was that he should never have let that lady with the red gloves feed him dog treats. When she had opened the garden gate, he had thought she was meant to be there, especially when she had the same dog treats that Emily used for when he did well at dog-training. She'd called him, and known his name, and the dog treats smelled so good – but he should have known! *She* didn't smell right, and then she'd grabbed his collar, and hauled him out of the garden and shoved him in the boot of that big car. Sam had barked, and tried to tell Jack to get help, but Jack had just watched, looking confused. The really scary thing was, he didn't know how to get out of this pen, or the big wooden shed where he and all the other dogs were shut in. He didn't know how he was supposed to get out and find Emily again. All he could do was call her – but how was she ever going to hear him?

Emily was finding it hard to believe that Sam had gone. She kept expecting to see him pop out from behind the sofa, with his tail whirling round and round, as if it was all just a silly game.

Every evening after school, she, Mum and Jack went out searching for Sam. Emily had used the computer to make some posters, with one of her favourite photos of Sam, and she'd put their phone number underneath.

LOST!
Sam
Golden Labrador puppy
Please help us find him!
Tel. 3826

They went into all the shops on the high street and asked if they could put them up in the window. Most of the shop people were happy to help, but no one phoned. Emily put one up at school too, and told everyone to look out for Sam. Some of her friends took posters to put in their windows as well.

Even with all this to do, the week seemed to drag on for ever. The policeman had promised he'd be in touch if there was any news, but it had been obvious that he didn't think they'd be getting Sam back. Sam seemed to have vanished into thin air. Emily didn't care. She was not going to give up – how could she, when everywhere she looked in the house reminded her of Sam? His food bowl, his red lead, his basket. The worst thing was the Sam-shaped emptiness at the end of her bed every night.

On Saturday, Dad took Emily to dog-training. He'd been a bit surprised when she asked if they could go, but she explained that she wanted to warn everyone in the class to watch out for the dog-nappers, and ask them to keep an eye out for Sam too.

It was horrible walking into the park without Sam. Dad squeezed Emily's hand as they walked through the gate, and she blinked back her tears. She wouldn't be able to talk if she started crying.

Lucy, the instructor, looked confused when she saw them. She was obviously wondering where Sam was, and that made Emily want to cry even more. But when Dad explained, she gathered the class together.

"I'm afraid Emily's got some terrible news about her lovely puppy, Sam."

Emily gulped. "Sam's been stolen," she gasped out. Her voice was wobbling, but everyone looked so sympathetic, she took a deep breath and went on. "The police say there's a gang stealing puppies, so please, please don't let them get any of yours. And please look out for Sam – just in case." Then she really did start to cry.

Everyone gathered round, promising to search for Sam, and saying they were sure he'd be found. Lots of the dogs licked Emily lovingly. Eventually Dad said they should go, so Lucy could get on with the class.

Just as they were walking back to the gate, Emily stopped, her heart thudding. It was that couple again! They'd been watching the class.

"What's the matter, Emily?" Dad asked gently.

"It's those people! The ones who were asking all the questions about Sam!" Emily stared at them. They had the pointer with them again, and he was plodding along with his tail drooping. No one who really loved dogs could have a dog who was so unhappy, Emily thought. Wasn't it suspicious that Sam had disappeared just a couple of days after those people had been so interested in him? So keen to find out if he was a valuable pedigree dog? She glared angrily at the woman,

80

not caring if she was being rude. The woman caught her looking, and said something to the man. Emily was sure she looked guilty.

Suddenly Emily's breath caught in her throat. She tugged Dad's hand urgently. "Look! Look!" she managed to gasp.

"What is it?"

"She's wearing *red gloves*!" Emily hissed. "Don't you remember? Jack said the lady who took Sam had red gloves! It all fits, it was them, they're the dog-nappers!"

"Emily, I know you're upset, but you can't accuse someone of stealing Sam just because of their gloves." Dad sounded embarrassed. He was pretty sure the man and woman had heard what Emily said.

Emily watched furiously as the couple neared the gate. How could Dad not understand? It was so obvious!

The woman smiled sympathetically as they came past. "We heard some of the people from the dog-training class saying that your puppy had been stolen," she said, looking straight at

Emily. "I'm so sorry. He's a darling. I really hope you get him back."

The man shook his head. "I can't imagine how we'd feel if someone took Bertie."

They really sounded as though they meant it. Emily just stared at the ground. She felt so confused. She'd been sure that this was the lady Jack had described, but maybe Dad was right. Was it stupid to decide somebody was a dog-thief, just because they had red gloves?

Chapter Five

That night, it took Emily ages to fall
asleep. She sat up in bed, hugging her
knees and worrying to herself. What if
it *was* the suspicious couple who'd
taken Sam? It made her shudder,
thinking about him being with them.
They *seemed* nice – but then she'd seen
them be horrible to Bertie the pointer,
and there was just something about

them that felt wrong. Sam had definitely sensed it too, and people said dogs always knew. Anyway, shouldn't she do something? The problem was, what? She wondered about ringing the policeman, but honestly, why would he believe her? She didn't have any real proof, and she wasn't absolutely certain herself.

Eventually Emily dozed off, but she was still worrying in her sleep. She seemed to be able to hear Sam, and he was crying for her! It wasn't just Sam, either. Lots of dogs were barking and whining and scratching to be let out of their cages. Yes, they were shut up, and they were all so upset. Emily shuddered, kicking the bedclothes off. Those people were there again. They *had* stolen Sam, she was sure of it. Just at that moment, she woke up, gasping. She felt so scared. Without thinking, she reached down to the end of the bed to call Sam for a cuddle, and of course, he wasn't there. Emily sat there, shaking and crying quietly. She had to do something. She was certain now that the couple from the park were the dog-nappers. She just *knew*.

Now she had to work out what to do about it.

Somehow, it was easier to sleep once she'd made her decision, and Emily woke up feeling much better. But she wasn't really any closer to getting Sam back. The only clue she had was that she thought the dog-napping couple must live quite close, because she'd seen them on the way to school, and in the park. But how was that going to help? She couldn't wander the streets looking for them.

"I've seen them twice at dog-training," Emily muttered to herself. Maybe that would be the place to find them? Then she gulped. Of course! She'd seen them at dog-training because *that was where they found the puppies they were going to steal!* It was the perfect place to find lots of dogs, and have friendly chats with their owners. Most people at dog-training loved to talk about their dogs, and how special they were. They wouldn't think it was odd that a nice couple with their own dog were interested. They probably went round lots of different dog-training classes, so that people didn't make the connection.

A plan began to form in her mind. *Maybe if I went back to dog-training, they'll be there too, and I can follow them home*, Emily thought, excitedly. *And if I can find out where they're keeping Sam, Mum and Dad will have to believe me!*

Lucy had a Sunday class in the park

too, in the afternoon. Now she just had to work on Mum and Dad to get her there. She wasn't going to admit her real reason, there was no way her parents would let her go off "bothering those poor people". She could just imagine Dad saying it. No, she would have to be a bit sneaky.

It wasn't hard to sit in the corner of the sofa and look as if she was moping – Emily felt a bit better now she had a plan, but she could easily drag up miserable thoughts about Sam. She could hear Mum and Dad muttering in the background. They'd noticed!

"Ought to get out and get some fresh

air," she heard her dad murmur. He strode cheerfully over to the sofa and announced in an over-bright voice, "Time for a walk, you two!"

Jack looked up crossly from his toy cars. "Don't want to walk," he grumbled.

Dad's bouncy attitude didn't slip. "Football!" he half-yelled, making Jack jump. "Come on, grab the ball, grab your coats, we're going to the park!"

Emily shook her head in disbelief. How easy had *that* been? Maybe she ought to try being sneaky more often. Although it was a pity they had to take Jack too, especially a grizzly Jack who moaned about being cold all the way to the park.

Actually, having Jack in tow was probably a good thing, Emily thought to herself, as she watched Dad try to jolly Jack along as they kicked the ball about between them in the park. Dad was having to spend so much time getting Jack not to lie down on the grass and sulk, that he wasn't really watching her. "Just going to practise dribbling," she called. Gently, she kicked the ball over towards the dog-training class, pretending to be using a line of trees for markers. Jack was now jumping up and down, swinging from Dad's hand and howling.

Emily lurked behind a big chestnut tree with a fat trunk, and peered round at the dog-training class. The sight of so many beautiful dogs, lots of them only puppies, made her stomach lurch, and she felt her eyes go hot with tears again. She shook herself firmly. If she wanted to get Sam back, she had to *do* something. Crying wouldn't help.

Carefully, Emily watched the class. It was a cold February day, and hardly anyone had stopped to watch. A few people were gathered up at the far end – but it was hard to see... Then someone moved, and she spotted Bertie the pointer sitting sadly by the man, who was talking with another dog-owner. The woman was standing next to him, wearing her red gloves, laughing at something. They were there! It couldn't be a coincidence. Emily felt her fingers curl into fists at the sight of them chatting so nicely. They were probably trying to pick up information about a new dog to steal.

Suddenly, the man hauled on Bertie's lead, and they started to walk away from the dog-training area, waving to the people they'd been chatting with.

Emily watched in horror from behind her tree. Now what was she supposed to do? Her plan had only gone as far as getting to the park. Quickly, she looked back round the tree. Eeek! Now Dad and Jack were coming over. Jack's bottom lip was sticking out, but at least he wasn't yelling any more.

"Sorry, Emily," Dad said, still trying to be super-cheerful. "Come on then, Jack! Let's see if Emily can get the ball past us, hmm?"

Emily looked over at the class in panic. The couple were heading for one of the side gates to the park now. What was she going to do? There was no way she could convince Dad to follow them, and even if she said she wanted to go home, they wouldn't use that gate.

It was time for a desperate move. Emily made a big thing of running up to the ball, faking a couple of times to get Dad and Jack in the mood, then booted it completely the wrong way – over towards the gate.

"Whoops! Sorry!" she giggled breathlessly. "I'll get it!" She raced off after the ball, which was still rolling feebly. There was a clump of big bushes close to the gate, and Emily made a big thing of rooting about in them after the ball. Then she simply nipped through the bushes and out of the gate.

Dad was going to go mad when he worked out what she'd done, but right now Emily didn't have time to think about that.

She was going to rescue Sam.

Chapter Six

Emily threw a quick glance back over her shoulder as she set off out of the park. Jack was being difficult again, and Dad had his hands full. Good.

The couple with the pointer were about halfway down the road, walking quite slowly, and talking to each other. Bertie was plodding along beside them, his tail drooping between his legs.

Emily had never tried to follow anyone before, and she didn't really know what to do. She was pretty sure that they would recognize her if they saw her, so she needed to keep back out of sight. She jogged up to a nearby postbox and hovered behind it, jigging from one foot to the other nervously. As soon as Bertie's black-and-white tail disappeared round the corner at the end of the road, Emily raced after them, skidding to a stop just before the corner, and peering round, helpfully disguised by a large but prickly rose bush.

She went on following them, lurking behind lamp posts and parked cars. Luckily not many people were around, and when someone did walk past, she just pretended to be doing up her trainers. It was weird. Emily felt silly hopping about behind trees, but scared at the same time. If she really was following the dog-nappers, what would happen if they noticed her? They weren't going to be pleased to see her.

After about five minutes, Emily spied round the next corner and got a shock. They'd gone! Her heart thumping in horror, Emily dashed into the next street. She couldn't have lost them. This was her only chance, because once Dad caught up with her, she was going to be grounded for life.

Suddenly, she heard voices.

"Come on, you stupid dog," someone said crossly. It sounded as though they were in one of the front gardens.

Emily took a deep breath, trying to keep calm. Maybe the couple lived in one of these houses. Yes, that had to be it, because this was quite a long road. Unless they'd started running, they couldn't have got that far ahead of her.

The street was full of big, old houses, and most of them looked neglected and shabby, some with boarded-up windows, as though they were empty. The gardens had quite high front walls, about shoulder height for Emily. She ducked down and scurried along to where she'd heard the voice coming from. It was a house on the end of a row, with a path running down the side, full of old rubbish. The garden was overgrown with bushes, so she peeped round the gate, hardly daring to breathe in case someone heard the air hissing in and out of her mouth. It was only now that she was so close that Emily started thinking about what might happen if she got caught. The grumpy man yelling at poor Bertie, who'd stopped to do a wee and have a sniff around halfway up the garden path, made her realize how much she did *not* want them to know she was there. The houses nearby looked as though they might be empty, with broken windows and gardens that were even wilder than this one. Emily shuddered. No one was around to help her out.

At last the man and woman went inside and slammed the front door.

Emily was left crouching by the gate, feeling a bit stupid. She'd done it – found where the couple lived. But what was she supposed to do now?

In the back garden, the dogs heard the slam of the front door, and started to bark – wanting someone to bring them some food, wanting to go out for a run, wanting someone to stroke and cuddle and fuss over them. Woken from a miserable sleep on the ratty old blanket that was his bed, Sam barked too, calling Emily to come and find him. It had been at least five days since he'd seen her, but he was still sure she was going to come and find him. Almost sure, anyway.

The people who'd taken him weren't exactly cruel, but they didn't seem to like dogs very much. Sam couldn't understand why they wanted so many, when they never even stopped for a pat or a hug. The man just shoved the food bowls down twice a day, scowling, and the woman with the red gloves never came into the dogs' shed at all.

Sam missed Emily desperately. He was used to being loved, petted, talked to. Even when Emily was at school he had her mum and Jack. Now he had no one, and it was miserable. Surely Emily would come and find him soon?

Emily slumped down on to the pavement. "I'm so stupid," she muttered to herself angrily. She felt tears burning her eyes. She'd got all this way, and now she didn't have a clue what to do next. She was never going to get Sam back!

But just as she was rooting in her pocket for a tissue, Emily heard barking. Lots of barking, from the back of the house. There was no way that was just Bertie. It sounded like five or six different dogs, and one of them had to be Sam!

Emily took a deep breath and stood up slowly. The house had an alleyway running down the side, and the fence looked really old and wobbly. Perhaps there was a way she could get round to the back garden and find those dogs. Maybe she could even squeeze through the fence? She couldn't give up now she was so close!

Just as she was creeping along the fence, making for the alley, someone grabbed her shoulder. Emily froze, unable to move.

Then an irritatingly familiar voice chirped, "We found you, Emily!"

Jack!

And, more to the point, Dad. It was Dad who'd caught her, of course. Emily drew in a deep shuddering breath, and turned round. Dad was glowering down at her, the expression on his face half furious, half worried.

"Emily, what on earth are you doing?" he hissed. "You know you must never, ever go off on your own like that!" He sounded as though he was really having to hold himself back from shouting.

"Dad, please listen! I think I've found Sam!" Emily burst out. "That's why I ran off, I was following those people with the pointer, they live here."

Dad just stared at her, then at last he shook his head wearily. "Emily, how many times have Mum and I told you that those people had nothing to do with Sam being stolen? Look, I know you're desperate to find Sam, but you've just picked this silly idea out of nowhere. Now come on, we're going home."

It would have been better if he had yelled at her. Somehow, Dad's quiet, sympathetic, sad way of putting it seemed awfully right. It was just a silly idea. All her clever detective work suddenly seemed so babyish.

"OK," Emily muttered miserably. Then she looked round. "Where's Jack?" she asked.

Dad looked down at his hand, as though he expected Jack still to be holding it. "I don't believe this," he murmured, looking around wildly.

Suddenly Emily saw a flicker of bright green through the broken fence panels – Jack's coat. He was heading down the alleyway she'd been about to investigate. "He's there!" she said, racing after him before Dad could stop her.

Jack was crouched down by the fence, further down the alleyway. He was listening, with his ear up against a hole in the wood.

Dad grabbed him, but Jack pulled out of his arms. "No, Daddy! I've found Sam! I've found him!" He jumped round and round as Dad tried to hold on to him.

"Jack, it's just a dog barking, it's not Sam." Dad was trying hard not to sound too cross, as he knew how much Jack and Emily wanted to find Sam, but he was losing patience.

"It is! Emily, it is, isn't it? You won't be cross with me now, will you?" Jack grabbed Emily's hand and tugged at her hopefully. "Listen!"

Emily crouched down by the hole in the fence. "OK, I'll listen," she said, more to make Jack shut up than anything else.

On the other side of the fence, Sam barked with all his strength, hurling himself against the side of his pen. It was Emily! She'd come for him at last! The miserable tone of his barking changed to delight.

"Right, we're going home, now!" Dad snapped. "This is ridiculous. What if the people who live here come out and see you upsetting their dogs?" He took both their hands and started to walk back to the street. "Emily, I'm sorry, but this has to stop. Come on."

No! They were going! Sam scrabbled against the wooden shed with his claws, fighting to get out and chase after them. How could they leave him now when they were so close?

"Dad, it really does sound like Sam," Emily said desperately, pulling back. "Please! Listen, don't you think it could be him?"

"It is Sam!" Jack put in crossly. "You're not *listening* to me. I told you it was." He wrenched his hand out of

Dad's and shot back to the fence. "Just listen." He started to sing loudly, "Row, row, row your boat, gently down the stream… Come on, Sam!"

And from the other side of the fence, Sam joined in gladly, "Ruff, ruff, ruff-ruff-ruff!"

"It is! It is him! Oh, Dad, we've found him." Emily flung her arms round her dad and hugged him, then she ran to join Jack by the fence. "Sam, it's me! We're going to get you out!" Then she hugged Jack and lifted him off the ground.

Dad was looking at the fence as though it had just exploded. "I don't believe it," he muttered. "Emily, I'm so sorry, I should have listened to you before. That has to be Sam, it just has to be." He shook his head in amazement. "OK, well, we'd better see what we can do. We can't exactly walk up to the front door and ask for him back."

Emily looked up at him worriedly. "What are you going to do?"

Dad smiled down at her. "It's all

right. We'll get him out. We just need some help, that's all. I'm going to call Mum and get her to call the policeman who was in charge of the dog-napping case. I wouldn't be surprised if those other dogs we can hear were stolen too."

Ten minutes later, a police car drew up outside the house, and Emily and Jack ran to meet it. "Can you get them out? Please?" Emily gasped.

"Hey, stop! You! Come back!" Dad was still standing in the alley by the fence, and he waved at the policeman. "Look, there are people climbing over the back fence!"

He was right. The dog-nappers had seen the police car arrive and were trying to get away, struggling over the fence that led into another garden.

The policeman got on his radio at once, calling for backup to come and chase after them. "Well, they've definitely done something they don't want to be caught for," he said. "So, how did you end up here?" he asked Dad curiously.

"Emily." Dad gave a sort of resigned shrug. "She wouldn't give up, and I have to admit, she was right."

"Me too!" Jack shouted indignantly.

"Well, we had our suspicions about these people. They've been trying to sell puppies to a pet shop not far from here. But you beat us to it," the policeman said, grinning. "I've got a search warrant for this house. Know what that means?" he asked Emily.

Emily shook her head.

"It means I can go in and look around. I think we should start just about here, don't you?" he asked, walking up to the rickety old gate at one end of the fence. He picked up an old brick that was lying on the path, and broke the lock. "Back in a minute," he said.

Emily could hear the barking from inside the garden getting louder and louder. She was sure the dogs knew they were about to be rescued. "You remember Sam, don't you?" she asked anxiously, pulling a photo out of her pocket. She'd been carrying it around with her all week, and it was bent and grubby, but Sam was still unmistakeable.

"Don't worry," the policeman assured her. "I'll get him for you. Not that you need much help!"

Emily and Jack stood by the gate,

craning their necks to see into the garden. There was a big old shed up against the fence, and they watched as the policeman shoved the door open.

Then Emily gasped as a golden blur shot out of the door, hurtling towards her. Sam!

She sat on the grass, crying and laughing at the same time as Sam jumped all over her, not knowing whether to bark or lick, and trying to do both. At last he stopped, out of breath, and just curled himself into Emily's arms, his head tucked under her chin. He sighed contentedly. He was back where he should be.

Emily hugged him tightly. It was so wonderful to breathe the sweet doggy smell of his fur, and feel the warmth of him nuzzled in her arms. The strange tight feeling in her middle, all that fear that she'd never see him and cuddle him again had completely gone.

Emily stood up shakily, and smiled at Dad and Jack over Sam's head. "Come on. Let's take Sam home."

Look out for:

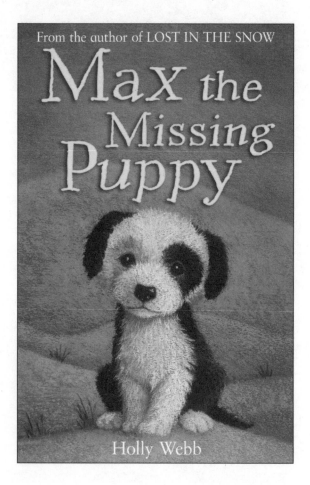

From the author of LOST IN THE SNOW

Max the
Missing
Puppy

Holly Webb

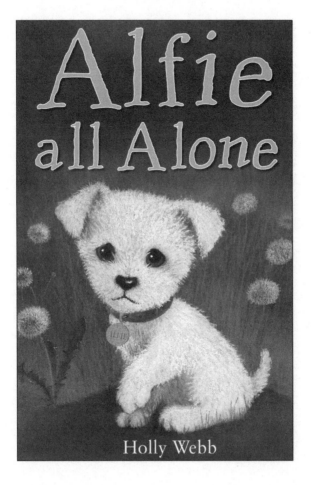

Alfie all Alone

Holly Webb

Lost in the Storm

Holly Webb

Animal Rescue
Tina Nolan

Abandoned … lost … neglected?
There's always a home at Animal Magic!

In a perfect world there'd be no need
for Animal Magic. But Eva and Karl
Harrison, who live at the animal rescue
centre with their parents, know that life
isn't perfect. Every day there's a new
arrival in need of their help!